Killer Apple Pie

A Pies and Pages Cozy

Mystery

Book One

BY

Carolyn Q. Hunter

Author's Note: On the next page, you'll find out how to access all of my books easily, as well as locate books by best-selling author, Summer Prescott. I'd love to hear your thoughts on my books, the storylines, and anything else that you'd like to comment on – reader feedback is very important to me. Please see the following page for my publisher's contact information. If you'd like to be on her list of "folks to contact" with updates, release and sales notifications, etc…just shoot her an email and let her know. Thanks for reading!

Also…

…if you're looking for more great reads, check out the Summer Prescott Publishing Book Catalog:

http://summerprescottbooks.com/book-catalog/ for

some truly delicious stories.

Contact Info for Summer Prescott Publishing:

Twitter: @summerprescott1

Blog and Book Catalog:

http://summerprescottbooks.com

Email: summer.prescott.cozies@gmail.com

And...look up The Summer Prescott Fan Page and Summer Prescott Publishing Page on Facebook – let's be friends! To sign up for our fun and exciting newsletter, which will give you opportunities to win prizes and swag, enter contests, and be the first to know about New Releases, click here:

https://forms.aweber.com/form/02/1682036602.htm

KILLER APPLE PIE

A Pies and Pages Cozy Mystery: Book One

TABLE OF CONTENTS

Prologue

"You're over six months late, Pennyworth," Kyle Jankes exclaimed, his booming voice echoing off the walls. He stood in the crowded office of Jefferson Street Booksellers, looming over the desk and glaring at the trembling old man sitting behind it.

The unsightly room reflected the shop owner's own life—cluttered and chaotic. Assorted boxes and stacks of books claimed dominion over large sections of the office.

"I really am sorry, Mr. Jankes, but I don't have the money right now," Brinkley Pennyworth offered a timid reply. He slid down into a hunched posture, lowering in the red woolen chair with each passing sentence. "I'm truly embarrassed about this, believe me," he confessed.

"Why shouldn't you be embarrassed? How difficult for you," Kyle snapped sarcastically.

"I swear, if I had the money, I would gladly give it to you right now."

Kyle slammed both palms down on the desk, sending a tremor through the room. A tall stack of books atop the desk wobbled slightly under the impact. "But you don't have the money, do you?" he shouted, emphasizing the word don't like an irritable adult speaking to a misbehaved young child.

"N-no. You're absolutely correct. I don't have the money."

"At one thousand and five-hundred dollars a month, do you know how much that is, Pennyworth?"

Brinkley paused, blinking with reddened wet eyes as he fiddled with his fingers, desperately attempting to do the math in his head.

"Nine thousand dollars," the answer ripped from Kyle's throat, his face turning red.

"Y-yes, it is, isn't it," he whimpered.

"Do you know what I could do with that money?"

"I think I do," he replied, a hint of defense in his voice.

"I could start up my own bookstore with that kind of cash."

"I'm not sure about that," Brinkley noted, trying to calculate the costs in his mind.

"I have this while strip of shops to worry about, the plumbing, the heating, the structure, constant repairs every month. These are old buildings, Pennyworth. They don't just keep themselves up."

"I know, I know," he sputtered, having slumped down to a slug's size in his desk chair.

"With all your late fees, you owe me an extra three hundred."

"I know," he continued repeating.

"And nine thousand three hundred dollars pays for an awful lot of repairs."

"I'm sorry, Mr. Jankes, I really am. I've just hit a bit of a rough spot, you see. Once things pick up again I can pay you back, any late fees included—the whole bit. Just give me another few weeks."

Kyle balled one hand into a fist and slammed it down onto the desk, rattling the tray of papers, the drawers of pens, the pile of keys and change, and toppling over the precariously stacked tower of books. They hit the floor with a thunderous crash. "No. I want you out of here by the end of the week, Pennyworth. No more chances. My charity can only be spread so thin."

"The end of t-this week?" he gasped.

"No questions, no delays. This whole place needs to be cleaned out. Do you hear me?"

Brinkley slumped down even further, lowering his chin to his chest and nearly disappearing behind the desk entirely. "This week? How can I get everything out in four days?"

"Three days. You need to be gone by Saturday morning."

"Three days," he blubbered, the tears finally rushing from his old gray eyes and creating zigzagging rivers in the wrinkles of his worn face.

Kyle let his fist untighten slightly and his rigid stance slacken. Sighing, he shook his head. His voice was calm and reserved for the first time that night. "I'm sorry, Brinkley, but I have no other choice."

"I-I understand." His words were drowned in tears, barely audible.

Kyle stood up and straightened the lapels of his dark suit jacket. "You have three days. Otherwise, I'll have you thrown out and all of your items sold at auction." Without waiting for another mumbled response, he turned and marched out of the office. The tinkling of the front doorbell declared his exit.

The shop was left in silence. Brinkley wallowed in his misery, throwing his head down upon the desk and weeping incessantly. His eyes watered the pile of mail beneath him, but he hardly cared.

He stayed that way for the next half-hour, crying until he felt he was all dried up.

Lifting his head from the desk and taking a breath, an envelope stuck to his hand and fell into his lap. Picking it up to toss back on the pile, he noticed that this wasn't an ordinary letter. In fact, it didn't have a stamp or return address on it. The only marker was the shop owner's name scribbled out in big letters.

While this had clearly been dropped through the mail slot earlier that morning, it certainly hadn't come through the normal channels.

Swallowing the lump in his throat, he used a long metal letter opener to rip the fold of the envelope—not doing a very good job of keeping it in a straight line.

Without even having read what the note said, Brinkley knew this could only be more ill news.

With shaking, bony fingers, he lifted the folded paper from inside and flipped the pages back to read it.

Pennyworth,

You still owe me nearly ten thousand on your recent "investment". If I do not see that money by Saturday night, I will be forced to take matters into my own hands. I will drop by your shop to see if you have the money.

Signed,

A Friend

With one final groan of despair, Brinkley tossed the paper aside onto the paper tray and threw himself face down onto the desk. His loud moans could easily be mistaken for a keening woman mourning her husband's death.

He stayed like that, weeping the rest of the night.

Chapter 1

There was nothing better in the world than pie, except for, perhaps, a good book. For Bertha Hannah, it was a constant battle for supremacy between the two. She was just thankful that she would never have to choose. At least, that was what she had thought during her normal morning routine that Wednesday in early August.

After fetching the newspaper off the driveway, she bustled about her small brick cottage home in Culver's Hood, Nebraska—brewed her daily blend of Ethiopian coffee, retrieved a lemon poppy seed muffin from the bread box, and sat down at the laminate table in her kitchen to drink in what the day had to offer.

After reading the comics, glancing over the cinema times to see what was playing, and doing the jumble puzzle (the only sections of the "news" worth worrying about) she finished up her breakfast and got right to work.

She needed flour, butter, sugar—both brown and white—shortening, cream of tartar, and the whole bushel of apples she had purchased at the market the Saturday before.

A woman of approximately sixty years of age, Bert was always finding ways to keep herself busy. Wednesdays, for instance, always included the same ritual of baking up a pie for the youth group at her church. All the young men and women of the congregation were wild fans of her famous, award-winning baking skills.

Most women would be proud to have won a few minor bake-offs at local fairs, school functions, and church activities. Bert, however, strived for so much more than that. Her pies had not only won the gratification of public praise, but had also been awarded the blue ribbon at the state fair along with a few delicious cash prizes—some reaching as high as a thousand dollars—at baking conventions and other similar events.

Still, even with all this well-earned success, Bert never let any of it go to her head. She enjoyed the praise, and of course enjoyed the cash prizes, but her real happiness came from the peace and solitude of baking.

Nothing could top the sensation of fresh flour against her hands, the satisfaction of cutting chilled butter into the dough, the bliss of rolling out a fresh crust, or the scent of sugar and apples mingling together.

Making a count of all the ingredients, just to make sure they were all there, Bert smiled and sipped on her second cup of coffee.

Glancing at the wood shelf above her sink, she reached up with a delicate hand, and brought down the cookbook titled 300 Percent Pie: 300 Pies for Every Occasion. Setting the book beside the sink, she began to fill a bowl with ice water to keep the butter chilled and ready for cutting.

She'd baked this pie so many times that she didn't need the recipe, but it was a force of habit, almost like a tradition, to consult the cookbook every now and again as she went about her work. Truth be told, part of this ritual was nostalgia. The book had belonged to her mother, and her grandmother before that. No other book came close to this one as far as quality or quantity, and Bert felt lucky to have it since it was out-of-print.

Now that she had the ice bowl filling, all the ingredients in place, and the cookbook at the ready, there was only one minor element missing to her normal pie baking pattern.

Walking over to the old cathedral style radio—a replica of the same one her grandparents had used while she was growing up—she turned the switch onto her usual station, The Night Club. The velvety sounds of a saxophone with the back-up of a big band filled the small kitchen. It was the perfect start to the day's baking process.

She paused one moment, closing her eyes and imagining her late husband standing there with her. In her mind's eye, he was a young man again. His beautiful head of auburn hair was back, combed neatly to one side. He was in his best suit, the one he used to wear to take her out. Howie held out a hand expectantly, and Bert graciously accepted—almost able to feel the warmth of his skin against hers.

Imagining his embrace, she danced across the kitchen of her own accord, the room dissolving into an elegantly decorated ballroom. They didn't have ballrooms like that anymore, at least not in Culver's Hood, Nebraska. She held her hand out as if she were holding Howie's and kept her arm around the invisible man's waist. Spinning in a circle, she prepared to do a little dip, but instead felt her hand smack into something on the counter.

There was a loud splash and a spray of cold water, all of which caused the memory to fade away like the fresh paints of an oil picture running off the canvas.

"Oh, my goodness," she sputtered. The cookbook had taken a nose dive, spine first, into the sink. Releasing a mild swear word, an old habit she'd picked up from her deceased husband, she quickly retrieved the cherished book from its watery grave.

"Oh, no. No, no, no." Holding it delicately, she tried to shake the water from the damp pages.

It was too late. The old worn paper was soaking up the liquid like a fresh sponge out of the package. The volume had almost doubled in weight and all the pages were sticking together in one large soggy mass.

"Maybe if I can just open it," she whispered to herself, wondering if it was possible to dry out her most cherished cookbook. Much to her horror, however, as she tried to pull apart two of the page, they began to tear, weakened beyond repair by the water damage.

Sighing in desperation, she placed the book on the counter with a gentle, almost reverent touch.

"So, much for that," she said half-heartedly.

While this little accident in no way had any real hindrance on her ability to whip up the pie, it just wouldn't be the same—and it most certainly wouldn't feel right—without that cookbook.

Where on earth was she going to get another copy? It was long out-of-print and there hadn't been any updated versions ever released.

After a moments consideration, she picked up the phone from the wall and prepared to call Pastor Chimney. She would just have to tell him she couldn't bake the pie for that evening's activities, not without the book. He would be disappointed, as would the teens, but there was no helping it. Bert was a woman who liked things to be just so, and if one element was out of place she simply felt she couldn't move forward with her plans.

Before she dialed the number, however, she paused. An idea had popped into her head.

She hadn't considered it right away because she'd been so upset over her careless behavior that led to the accident, but maybe she could find a copy of the book. It was a long shot, but there was a used bookshop in the historical Old Market downtown. It was just possible they might have a copy tucked away in the stacks.

A smile of determination returning to Bert's face, she quickly pulled on her light denim jacket, grabbed her keys, and walked out the front door.

Chapter 2

I t wasn't her usual routine to visit the Old Market in the middle of the week. Bert generally reserved her outing to the historic downtown district of Culver's Hood for Fridays. Her schedule was nearly always the same: First, she would pay a visit to her best friend Carla Young at the Christmas in July shop. They sold ornaments, miniature villages, and all manner of decorations year-round. Second, she stopped in next door to the Candy Emporium where she'd buy her favorite ice cream cone, Cherry Chocolate Swirl. Last, but not least, she'd visit Brinkley Pennyworth at the used bookshop. She always spent the rest of the afternoon there, sitting in a secluded corner and reading a new book she had purchased.

This series of events was something she'd begun doing on a weekly basis after Howie had passed away. It was a treat to herself, and helped to ease the pain of missing him—even after five years.

Today, however, her plans were much different, and she quickly found a parking spot on the cobblestone street in front of Jefferson Street Booksellers. Paying the meter with a single quarter, she headed through the glass door on the right. There was a second door on the left, originally part of a separate storefront which had eventually been bought and combined with the bookshop, but it had been blocked off with a large bookcase.

In her hurry, Bert didn't notice the pink slip hanging from the window declaring a going-out-of-business sale on every single item in the store. Eighty percent off any book you could lay your hands on. Bert was a woman with a goal and needed to be in and out without so much as a hiccup.

The store had shelf after shelf, all floor to ceiling, of old books waiting to be snatched up by eager buyers. The aisles and walkways between shelves were small, but cozy, and there were several nooks and crannies where a plush chair or floor cushion had been set up for private reading.

Bert headed straight toward the front checkout counter, which had a long wooden staircase leading up to a balcony and second floor, and got in line.

There was only one man in front of her, and she patiently waited to speak with Brinkley. She took notice that the stranger seemed angry, his voice strained as he spoke.

"Didn't you get my note I sent you yesterday, Pennyworth?" the man was demanding.

"I-I did, Marc. Honest, I did."

"Then tell me. Why weren't you prepared when I came in today?"

"The letter said I had until Saturday. It's only Wednesday."

"You think I don't know what day it is?" the man snapped, a slight New York accent coming through.

Bert leaned forward, not wanting to intrude, but interested in what exactly was going on here. The stranger wore his shimmering blonde hair in a ponytail. A neatly trimmed beard gave him the look of a Viking. In contrast to the hairstyle, he wore a well-tailored pair of slacks and a button up red shirt with a black tie.

"Marc, I'm up to my neck in it already. I just don't have the money today."

"What about this joint? I'm sure your business is worth something, at least. Why not sell it?"

Bert let out an audible gasp. Brinkley sell the bookshop? That just didn't seem right.

The man, whose name was Marc, glanced back briefly at the older woman behind him, but ultimately ignored her outburst.

"I'm telling you, Marc, I'm working it out. Didn't you see my sign in the window?"

Bert glanced at the door and noticed the pink sign for the first time. Despite the lettering being backwards from the inside of the shop, she couldn't help but feel sick in her stomach. Was one of her favorite shops closing their doors forever?

"And you think selling a few measly books at a discount is going to save you? I recommend you think about more drastic decisions here, my friend, otherwise, I can't guarantee what will happen."

Was this man threatening Brinkley? Bert considered going out into the street and finding one of the historic market's security officers— an official brand of the Culver's Hood police—and getting them to intervene.

"Please, please, I'll have it by Saturday. I swear."

The man paused, leaning on the counter with a sneer on his upper lip. "I'll be back. I hope you have a better answer for me when I arrive." Turning around, Marc barreled his way out of the store, almost pushing Bert over as he went along. He didn't even bother apologizing for bumping her, acting as if she was just an inanimate object in his way.

"Bert, h-hi," Brinkley said, his face turning red with embarrassment.

"Are you okay?" she asked, stepping up to the counter and placing a gentle hand on her friend's arm. She knew he was a quiet, mild-mannered man—not the sort of person you'd ever see standing up for themselves.

"I'm sorry you had to see all of that. It was nothing, really."

"It didn't sound like nothing. This Marc fellow seems like bad news."

Brinkley could only shrug in reply. "It's my fault, I suppose."

"Are you in some sort of trouble?" she asked, her womanly instinct to help solve the problem kicking in.

"Naw," he smiled, drawing his arm back from her.

Tilting her head to one side, she raised a scolding eyebrow.

The shop owner licked his lips. "Well, I may have made a few bad investments that are catching up to me."

"It's bad enough to close the shop? I mean, I saw the sign. You have to sell all your merchandise and close down to pay off these . . . debt collectors?" she asked, glancing toward the doorway again.

Brinkley swallowed a heavy lump in his throat. "Unfortunately, Bert, yes. I'm sad to say it's true."

"But surely there's another answer."

"Trust me, Bert. If there had been another way, I would have found it already."

Bert quickly had her purse on the counter and began digging around for her checkbook. "Surely there is something we can do. Maybe I can loan you a little money, just to get you past this rough patch. I have some savings built up. I was going to maybe use it for a European vacation or something, but this is more important." She found what she was looking for and set it out. Pulling a pen closer to her, she poised it at the ready. "How much do you need?"

The elderly gentleman's eyes were beginning to mist, a sure sign that this was no little thing. "It isn't only Marc. I've got Mr. Jankes breathing down my throat, too."

"Mr. Jankes? Who's that?" she pressed.

"He's my landlord for this space. I'm six months behind on my payments to him."

"Six months? How much money is that?"

Brinkley couldn't bring himself to look at her, his wet eyes staring off into space. "Over nine thousand."

Bert's jaw dropped.

"And it's even more than that for Marc," he whispered, completely ashamed of his current situation.

She realized she wasn't breathing, the air caught in her lungs while she struggled for a new answer to this problem. She wanted to say something, anything, to help fix this, but her mind was a blank.

Before she could finish formulating any sort of new idea or plan, a voice interrupted their pained silence.

"Excuse me, sir?" said an older woman. She had her hair permed in a fashionable manner, and clutched a small purse delicately in her hands.

Brinkley quickly blinked any tears away, trying to hide them from this customer. "Yes, Pearl, what can I do for you?"

Bert noted how he called the woman by her first name, indicating that she was probably a regular just like Bert.

"I saw that you were going out of business. Does that mean all of the books are on sale here?"

"Yes. Yes, that is right. Any book you can find is eighty percent off."

"Very good," she beamed.

"Was there something specific you were looking for?"

"As a matter-of-fact, there is." She pointed toward an old tome sitting behind the counter, displayed on a little wooden tripod. "I've always loved that book right there, the copy of Macbeth. How much will you take for that?"

"O-Oh," Brinkley stuttered, a rush of embarrassment turning his ears red.

"Well?" she pressed.

"I spoke out of turn a second ago when I said every book was on sale. It was misleading. This book is not for sale."

"Well, why the devil not?" she exclaimed, her shaky voice raising an octave.

"This belonged to my great-grandfather. It is sort of a family piece, you understand."

The woman, not listening to his explanation in the slightest, dug into her purse and retrieved a fifty-dollar bill. "I'll give you fifty for it. Will that be enough?"

"Oh, no ma'am. You don't seem to understand. I have a nostalgic attachment to this book. It can't be sold."

Bert completely understood where Brinkley was coming from. While it wasn't worth much, the pie cookbook that had belonged to her mother and grandmother was something she was unwilling to ever part with—not on purpose anyways.

Pearl grunted, flattening her lips together. Digging into her purse again, she came out with another twenty. "Fine, I'll give you seventy for it, but that's my final offer."

"It's not for sale, I'm sorry," he shook his head.

She fished out another twenty. "Ninety, then."

Bert cut in, knowing that Brinkley wasn't always the best at standing his ground. "Ma'am, he told you it's not for sale. Now, why don't you find a different book to buy?"

"And who the devil are you?" she snapped, turning on Bert.

"An old friend of Mr. Pennyworth. Please respect the shop owner and select a different book."

"This is ridiculous," she shouted, shoving the money haphazardly back into her purse.

"I'm very sorry about this, Ma'am," Brinkley offered.

"Absolutely ridiculous. You're both just trying to make me upset." Pulling her hand out of the purse again, she revealed an orange pill bottle.

"Are you interested in something else, perhaps?" he asked, trying to smooth the waters.

"No," she shouted, popping two pills in her mouth and swallowing them dry. "I want that book," she demanded, pointing at the copy of Macbeth.

"I'm sorry, no," he said.

"Fine," she grumbled, stomping her way toward the door. Stepping outside, she tried to slam the door shut, but the spring kept it from closing. Letting off a final huff of defiance she disappeared down the cobbled street.

Chapter 3

"She's a regular?" Bert asked once the woman was out of sight.

"Unfortunately so. Pearl Wright is her name. She's an avid book collector and had always been sort of a needy customer." He groaned and looked toward the window.

"Has she showed interest in that book before? Macbeth, I mean."

"Only once, the first time she came in. I told her it wasn't for sale and she had a similar reaction. Since then, she's known it wasn't for sale. I guess today, since I'm going out of business, she assumed it was up for grabs."

Bert scrunched up her nose in distaste. "How can people act like that? Entitled and all."

He shook his head and leaned on the counter in a mournful way. "On the bright side, I won't be stuck dealing with people like her anymore."

"Now just hold on. Surely there is something we can do to keep this place going," Bert offered, still desperate for an answer to this problem.

"No, I'm afraid not, Bert. I'm getting up there in years. Maybe it's just time to close down, get out of the business for good."

"How can you say that?"

"I'm getting too old for all of this. It just took something drastic like money problems to make me realize the truth and give me that push out the door." He looked around himself, at all the many stacks of books, the shelves, the reading chairs, everything. "It's just a shame that the whole store has to go down with me."

Bert was quiet for a moment after what the store owner said, strange and crazy ideas forming in her head. What she was thinking was impossible, ludicrous even, but she had the uncanny desire to act on a whim.

In a life filled with order and routine, Bertha Hannah was about to step out of her comfort zone.

"Maybe," she hesitated, almost afraid to say it. "Maybe, I could buy the business from you."

* * *

"Bert! Land sakes, what are you doing here? It isn't Friday," Carla Young exclaimed in joyous accord upon seeing her best friend walk through the front door of Christmas in July. The little shop, decorated to the hilt in yuletide festivities, had the sound of Silver Bells playing over the speakers. Carla was a loud and boisterous woman who had curly reddish-silver hair and bright red lipstick that framed her smile. She looked like a nineteen-fifties housewife version of Mrs. Claus in her red and white patterned dress and matching frilly apron.

Bert was sure it was all on purpose. "Hi, Carla. How's business?" she asked, walking over to the glass counter which contained various expensive antique ornaments and miniature Christmas houses.

"A little slow, but good none-the-less."

"A little slow? Tell me you're not thinking of closing shop," Bert teased, wondering if this day could have any crazier surprises.

Carla blinked, clearly confused. "Why in the world would you think we were closing shop?"

"No reason," Bert smiled, leaning on the glass case as if she were eager to share some big news.

Carla tilted her head and smirked. "What is it? What's going on?" she asked in a sing-song voice.

"I haven't the faintest idea what you're talking about," Bert played dumb.

"Come on, don't leave me in the dark," she patted her friend's hand eagerly.

"Leave you in the dark? I'm not leaving you in the dark."

Carla grabbed Bert by the shoulders. "Do I have to shake it out of you, woman?" she joked, eager and insistent on hearing this news her friend was keeping hidden.

"Okay, okay, I'll spill," she laughed.

"What? What is it?"

"Well, you know the bookstore just on the next street."

"Jefferson Booksellers?"

"That's the one," she tapped the glass case.

"What about it? Did you find an awesome new book to read? Do I get to borrow it?"

She shook her head, holding back the laughter. "Nope. You're way off. You're never going to guess."

"Then just tell me," she begged.

Pausing for effect, Bert leaned in close to her friend, and then proclaimed, "I'm going to buy it."

There was another pause, but this one was in confusion. "What do you mean?"

"Exactly what I said."

"You're buying something?"

"I'm buying the bookshop."

"What?" Carla cried, her smile fading and complete shock coming over her face.

"That's right. I'll be taking over for Brinkley."

"Wait, you bought Jefferson Booksellers?"

Bert tilted her head to one side. "Well, I haven't bought it yet. I will get to the bank later today and see Mr. Cartwright about a loan. I mean, I've been a customer with him my entire adult life and have always managed my loans and mortgages responsibly. I think it should be easy."

"But, you're going to buy it?" Carla asked for clarification.

"That's right."

"I can hardly believe it. How long have you been planning this and not telling me?"

"Planning? There was no planning," she admitted.

"What?"

"I just made an offer today on a whim."

There was an odd pause and then Carla began laughing. "You just decided on a whim to buy the bookshop? You? Bertha Hannah?"

"Is that so hard to believe?" she defended herself, placing her hands on her hips and scowling at her friend.

"It's just surprising, is all." Carla continued giggling.

"It shouldn't be. I do crazy things occasionally."

Carla shook her head. "No, you don't. Everything in your life is meticulously planned."

"Not everything."

"Yes, it is."

Bert sighed, dropping her scowl and giving a smile. "Guess you're right. I'm a creature of habit, I suppose."

"That's why I was so surprised to see you walk in. It isn't Friday. I thought you would be at home today baking up pies for the youth function at church tonight."

Carla and Bert were two friends who'd originally met at church, but when Howie had passed on, they'd become closer than ever. For Bert, Carla was like her advocate.

"Oh shoot. I was so caught up in all this excitement that I completely forgot."

"You forgot it was Wednesday?" she gasped, hardly able to contain her surprise.

"Hardly. The whole reason I came down here in the middle of the week is because I foolishly destroyed my favorite cookbook."

"Oh, no. Your mother's?"

She nodded. "I'm afraid that's the one. I knocked it into a bowl of water and now it's unusable. I simply cannot bake without that book."

"Sure, you can. You know all the recipes by heart."

"You don't understand. It's part of the routine. I just can't do it."

Carla smirked and shook a knowing finger. "That's the Bert I know and love."

"I know it'll be a real hassle for the pastor, but I'll just call and inform him he'll have to do store bought ice cream sandwiches for the kids tonight."

"I'm sure they'll understand. Just don't tell them it's because your cookbook was ruined. I'm not sure they'll believe you."

"And why not?"

"Because not everyone knows about your little quirks like me, that's why."

"I suppose you're right," she agreed, looking at a little miniature school inside the glass case. It had a glass pond out front with tiny children skating on it. "Either way, I still need a copy of that book if I can get my hands on it."

"When do you sign the paperwork?"

"I'm meeting with both Brinkley and Mr. Jankes after the shop closes on Friday."

"Oh, Mr. Jankes is such a nice man. He's the landlord over my shop, too."

"Brinkley didn't seem to think Jankes was nice, but I guess I couldn't blame the man for being angry. After all, rent hasn't been paid up on that shop for a few months."

"Is that what happened? Brinkley isn't getting enough business to keep it up?"

"I guess not. It seems like he owes quite a bit of money around," she informed her friend.

Carla took a seat on the stool she had behind the counter and thought pensively. "That worries me a little. If Brinkley can't bring in enough business to stay afloat, you'll seriously have to look at making some changes to the way he's been doing things, otherwise, you'll just go under as well."

"I don't know about that. I think he just spread himself a bit too thin for too long, is all. I know I've done that myself when I was trying to bake for every church function, for state competitions, and for school fundraiser activities this last summer."

Carla's eyes widened with delight, an idea brewing. "Pies!" she exclaimed.

"What about pies?"

"I've got it. I know how you can revitalize that bookstore. Everyone loves your pies, right? They've even won tons of competitions?"

"Yes, that true. What are you saying?"

"What I'm saying is, why not combine your two passions—pies and books?"

Bert suddenly began to catch on, her face lighting up. "Wait, you mean turn it into a sort of pie shop meets a bookstore?"

"Exactly!"

She was already imagining the possibilities. "I could easily clear out that left side, the one that used to be a separate shop, and turn it into the pie side of things. It can have tables, plush chairs and couches, a perfect setting to enjoy a slice of heavenly pie and read a new book."

"Brilliant, brilliant, brilliant!" Carla clapped her hands with a new eagerness.

"I just thought of a name for it, too," Bert gleamed with delight at the idea.

"Tell me."

Bert looked upwards, imagining the new sign on the freshly renovated shop. "Pies and Pages."

Chapter 4

"It's a pleasure to meet you, Mr. Jankes," Bert offered her hand in greeting to the younger man. He was tall, slender, and had an old-fashioned flair of etiquette about him. His dark business suit and carefully trimmed hair added to an overall professional vibe.

He gladly took her hand and shook it with a firm grip. "The pleasure is all mine, Mrs. Hannah. If we can work out something here that will help both you, me, and Mr. Pennyworth, I'm thrilled to talk business."

"As am I. Brinkley being an old friend of mine. If we can keep him upright, I am more than happy to offer a helping hand."

"It's about time someone took over the business, anyway," Brinkley added with an honest smile, something he hadn't been able to do for months. "Shall we all adjourn to the office?" He motioned for them to follow and led the way into the cramped back room of the bookstore.

"Whew, it's warm in here," Bert admitted, taking a seat on a wooden chair in front of the desk. Kyle sat in the seat next to hers.

"Yes, you'll have to forgive me, but I always shut the vent when I'm working back here." He pointed up at the ceiling. An old metal grate was situated directly above the desk.

"Why is that?" she asked.

Brinkley set down a file folder full of paperwork on the desk. "I keep a lot of papers and other similarly light items out here." He indicated the multilevel paper tray, his sticky notes, his pens, a long silver letter opener, and his pile of pocket items—keys, wallet, loose change, a stick of gum, and even a little lint. "Whenever I leave that vent open, the wind comes in from outside and blows all my things around and makes a mess, so I preemptively closed it for tonight. I didn't want any of this important paperwork to get messed up." He tapped the brown folder.

"These are old buildings, Mrs. Hannah. Sometimes these things can be a little finicky. However, what you lack in modern amenities is made up with the charm of having a shop in the official historic Old Market," Kyle added his two cents worth on the matter.

"I couldn't agree more," she smirked.

"Shall we get down to business?" Kyle asked, motioning to Brinkley.

"Of course," he said, taking a seat behind the desk. "I had all these papers drawn up this afternoon by my lawyer, whom I also owe a small sum. Still, with the knowledge that I would be getting money out of this deal to pay him, he agreed to help me out."

"Shall we go over the basics?" Kyle suggested.

"A good idea. These papers, at their very simplest, transfer my entire business, all the merchandise, shelves, and material here in the store to you. In the end, we sign the papers and I walk off leaving everything as is for you."

"Crystal clear so far," Bert said.

"Also, you'll take over my lease here with Mr. Jankes. I'll remain responsible for the money I owe to him for the months I've been here, but will no longer be held accountable for future payments, including this month of August."

Kyle only smiled and nodded.

"Sounds alright to me," she asserted.

"Did you get a chance to read over the agreement I sent you earlier?" Kyle asked.

"I read your e-mails and it all seems very fair," she agreed.

"In the end, there will be only one item that I keep from the shop."

Bert held up a finger for him to stop. "Let me guess. Your family heirloom?"

He chuckled slightly. "That's the one."

"I feel that is very agreeable," she said.

"As do I," Kyle added. "Now, there is one other thing I want to know before we sign anything. This shop has been struggling for some time now. Mrs. Hannah, what makes your business plan different? Do you have a vision to change things up so that the business becomes profitable again?"

"I do have a plan, in fact," she told him with a wide smile. Instantly, she started into her practiced speech she'd prepared and memorized. It was the same one she'd used at the bank when discussing the possibility of a business loan. She talked about all the ins and outs of Pies and Pages. "Not only will it be a combination pie shop and bookstore, but we are going to start selling new merchandise as well, new books by up-and-coming authors. This will allow for lower prices on the used books."

"I have to admit, Mrs. Hannah, I'm in love with your idea. I think adding the food element is an excellent idea."

"Thank you very much," she smirked, feeling proud of her business plan.

"However, I still have my concerns."

This came as a small blow to Bert. She'd worked hard on her presentation and had made sure it was perfect. She had wowed the loan specialist with it, so what was wrong now? "Oh?" she asked, trying to remain polite.

"You seem like a capable woman, but do you have any experience in business? How do I know you'll be able to handle a venture of this magnitude?" he asked.

She nodded, carefully formulating her answer. "It's an honest question, but I can assure you that I know my way around. My late husband ran a successful carpet laying business for over thirty years, and I was always the one to balance the books."

"And what has happened to this business?"

"When my Howie passed on, I sold the company for a considerable sum which I have in a savings account. So, you see, I not only have an upcoming loan from the bank for this venture, I also have the extra capital to give this location the real renovation and spark it needs."

Kyle couldn't help but smile with utter satisfaction. "You certainly seem like a woman who knows what she's doing."

"I am that, thank you," she agreed.

"In that case, I have no other qualms or questions." He motioned to the file folder on the desk. "Shall we sign the papers?"

* * *

Once they'd completed the deal, Kyle and Bert stood up and prepared to leave for the night. It was already nine and they'd been sitting for a couple hours going over the details.

"Here is your key," Brinkley held out the brass key.

"Thank you very much," she said, graciously taking it. She felt somewhat powerful holding the key and knowing the shop was officially hers.

"I am truly grateful to you. With this money from selling the business, I'll be able to finally pay off my debts."

"And we are all thrilled to know that," Kyle laughed, patting Brinkley on the back.

"Now, I've kept a copy of the key. I'll finish closing up tonight and take a few moments to say goodbye if you don't mind."

"I don't mind at all," Bert noted, completely understanding the need to have rituals in life.

"When I'm done, I'll lock up the place and then slip the key through the mail slot for you."

"Perfect," she replied, forming her thumb and index finger into an "O" shape. "I hope to see you around still."

He nodded with a smile. "Trust me. You will."

With that, they all shook hands one more time, and Bert and Kyle headed out into the night, walking in separate directions to their cars.

Chapter 5

Bert woke up the next morning with a delighted anticipation, a sensation she hadn't felt since Howie was alive. Sliding out of bed and going about her usual routine, she could hardly contain her excitement. Her hands were shaking and she couldn't wait to get into the shop and get down to work.

There was a lot of planning to do, a lot of cleaning, and a lot of moving. Luckily, she knew, when it came time to clear out the left side of the shop, a few of the young men from the church would be willing to help move items back and forth for her. Boxes of books weren't exactly light, after all.

Unusual as it was, Bert skipped reading the newspaper that morning and instead grabbed her coffee and muffin and headed out the door.

She was already keenly aware that she was going to have to change her usual morning schedule around slightly. While the bookstore never opened until ten in the morning, and Bert intended on keeping those hours, the new pie aspect to the shop would require her or other employees she hired to arrive early and start preparations for the day's menu items.

As she drove away from her cottage home, she formulated plans in her mind about how the menu would work. She knew that there should always be a few well-known staples available: apple, cherry, lemon, coconut, chocolate, and a few more she hadn't settled on yet. She might even set them on a rotating daily schedule throughout each week.

On top of the regulars, she decided she would also do weekly specials, delicious new pies for patrons to try and enjoy.

However, pies weren't the only thing on her mind. There were, of course, books as well. She had a plethora of wonderful ideas about how to bring the local writing community together with readers. Signings, readings, children's hour, book clubs, and so much more were on the table as fantastic new ways to interest the public in the store.

It was all so thrilling she could taste it already. Also, being just around the corner from her best friend's Christmas shop was an added bonus.

Bert finally arrived at the Jefferson Street Booksellers and parked. Getting out, she breathed deeply.

The streets of three-story brick buildings really made this part of town seem like something preserved in time. The cobblestone streets mixed with the classic storefronts. The wrought iron street lights–which looked just like old gas lamps—created an ambiance she had always loved.

It was why she'd been so drawn to it all these years. Many of the shops even had the gothic style iron fences out front or around concrete stairways that led down to basements or kitchens where the hired help used to go in and out.

She was happy to see that she could also see the main square and Old Market Gardens at the middle of the historic district.

When spring rolled around the following year, there would be beautiful blooms to see.

Breathing in deeply, she took in all the excitement and beauty. It all seemed serendipitous. Even though it was against her usual nature to just make such a big decision on the fly, she couldn't help but feel it was meant to be.

It was a dream come true.

Finally turning to her new shop, she unlocked the door, which was firmly latched, and stepped inside. Glancing down at the entrance mat where patrons could wipe their feet, she looked for the key.

However, after some inspection, it appeared that the key wasn't there at all.

"He must have just forgotten to slip it through," she said out loud, confident he would come back whenever he realized he still had it and give it to her. It was no problem.

Setting her purse on the counter, she took in the cluttered, yet cozy atmosphere of the store around her.

That was when she noticed a light still on in the office, seeping through the crack of the slightly open door and casting a line through the dim shop.

"He is forgetful," she complained, heading through the stacks to the back. He'd not remembered to return the key or turn off the light before he locked up and left the night before.

Opening the office door, she grabbed the switch to turn it off.

However, before she could plunge the room into darkness, she froze stiff, staring at the strange and unexpected sight presented before her. Leaning back in the office chair, his eyes wide open in a death stare, was the dead body of Brinkley Pennyworth—a bloody wound seeping through his nice white shirt.

Bert screamed.

Chapter 6

Bert sat in the upstairs break room at Christmas in July with a steaming cup of coffee in her hands and a warm, freshly made donut sitting on a napkin in front of her—both from a local café and compliments of her dear friend Carla.

The police detective placed in charge of the case took control the instant he was on the premises—and that included sweeping Bert aside for the time being.

Detective Harold Mannor seemed like a stiff, by-the-rules kind of guy, and had somewhat poor bedside behavior when it came to situations like this. He'd been firm, but demanding in his assertion that Bert wait for him to finish up preliminary investigations before he would ask her any questions.

He preferred that she not remain inside the shop while they did their initial walk-through for evidence. Bert suggested she go and stay at a friend's shop until he was ready to talk to her.

"Just don't go too far. I don't want to end up having to track you down if you decide to run off," he warned her in his husky voice.

She didn't like the sound of his tone and already knew she was being considered as one of the suspects. Still, she gladly left to find her dear friend at the Christmas shop.

She'd been in a state of horror upon her arrival, but had finally managed to take a few deep breaths and calm down. Thankfully, the Christmas carols playing on the radio were rather helpful in this regard.

"I just can't imagine finding someone like that," Carla noted, taking a seat at the table with her friend, her own cup of coffee in hand. The mug she was using was red with a white rim to look like snow.

"The whole thing doesn't seem quite real, yet," Bert admitted.

"Do the police really think it was murder?"

Bert looked her in the eye. "If you'd seen what I had, you'd believe it was murder."

Carla shivered. "Spooky. How did he die?"

"I'm not positive, but I think he was stabbed with something. That's what it looked like."

"Stabbed? Oh heavens, with what?"

"I didn't stick around very long to find out, would you?"

Carla nervously bit her bottom lip. "I suppose I wouldn't."

"Anyway, I don't remember seeing a darn thing. No knife, no weapon of any kind. I mean, it isn't like that room is totally clean and tidy, and neither was that desk."

Carla let out a loud gasp. "What if the killer hid it somewhere in there?"

"With the mess in there, it could take the police days to find it."

"Take us days to find what, exactly?" echoed a male voice from the doorway of the small break room. Detective Harold Mannor stood there in his knee-length gray trench coat, white shirt, and red tie. His badge clung to his coat lapel in a lopsided manner that bothered Bert. The detective was an older man appearing to be in his late sixties, and was the sort of fellow you'd expect to have retired already. Instead, he was standing there with his silver hair, a bulldog of a face, and a small cardboard box under one arm.

He was ready to ask some questions about the murder. "Well, what will take us days to find, Mrs. Hannah?" he reiterated his question.

"The murder weapon."

"Are you admitting to tampering with evidence?" he pressed, narrowing his eyes in an accusatory way.

"Certainly not," Bert defended herself.

Carla jumped in to her defense. "Bert was just saying that she didn't see any murder weapon on the scene when she found the body, and we both guessed it could be hidden among the storage boxes in that office."

"And you are?" he shot a glance at the second woman whom he'd not met yet.

"This is Carla Young, a good friend of mine and the owner of this shop," Bert informed him, not wanting her to get mixed up in all this murder business.

"I see," the officer said, raising a suspicious eyebrow. Without asking to be invited, he pulled out a chair and sat at the table, setting the cardboard box down next to him.

"Would you like a cup of coffee, Detective?" Carla asked.

"If you don't mind," he responded without so much as a please or thank you, never making eye contact with Carla. Instead, he had his gaze trained on Bert.

"Cream or sugar?"

"Black," he harrumphed.

Carla bowed slightly, not wanting to bother him any more than she already had since he seemed so annoyed. Walking across the room, she grabbed the carafe from beside the sink and poured a new cup.

The whole time, the detective stared at Bert.

Setting the pink, white, and red patterned Christmas mug in front of the officer, he picked it up and sipped from it—only stopping for a brief second to eye the cup's design with a twitching lip of distaste.

"Mrs. Hannah, do you know what this is?" he asked, holding up a small brass key that was identical to the one she had inside her purse.

"Brinkley Pennyworth's key to the building, I assume," she shrugged, not understanding why this was the first question out of the gate.

"And, exactly, how do you know it's a building key?"

"Easy, it's the same one I have to the building." Digging into her purse, she retrieved her key and placed it on the table next to her donut.

He eyed it with a curious gaze. "How, may I ask, did you get that key?"

"Brinkley gave it to me last night."

"He gave it to you?" the officer pressed with an inquisitive stare.

"Of course. I signed all the paperwork to buy the bookshop from him."

At this, Detective Mannor paused, scrunching his lips together. "You purchased the business?"

"Just last night. Mr. Jankes and I were there to take care of all the papers and to collect the key to the building."

"Mr. Jankes? Who is that?"

"Kyle Jankes. He's the landlord to a few different pieces of property here in Old Market," Carla chimed in.

The detective paused, clearly unamused with Carla's presence. "Mrs. Young, was it?" he asked, turning in his seat slightly.

"That's right."

"Would you please wait outside." It was a command, not a suggestion.

She paused, her mouth open slightly in shock. Bert knew that look. Her friend was offended. However, without a word of complaint, Carla was out the door, shutting it behind herself.

"There, a little more privacy," he grunted.

"She was telling the truth. His name is Kyle Jankes and he is the landlord."

"I don't doubt it. He has a key to the building as well, I presume."

"Of course. What landlord wouldn't have a key to their own building?"

The detective nodded and pulled out a notepad, scribbling down a few haphazard sentences.

"Do you mind telling me what's so significant about those keys?" Bert asked, curious as to what he was getting at.

"We found this on the desk in front of the victim," he tapped the brass key with his index finger.

"That isn't surprising. He kept many things on his desk."

"It was sitting in the middle of the desk, instead of one of his piles."

"Piles?"

He pulled the lid off the box and showed her the items inside. "There was a whole slew of items like these—wallet, change, a stick of gum, a loose breath mint, and his keys—sitting in a neat little pile to the side."

Bert noticed that the detective hadn't grabbed the pocket lint with it all, but examined the rest of the varied items.

"There were also some books, pens, and his paper organizer." He held up the shop key. "However, this wasn't in any of the piles. It was just sitting there right in the center of the desk in front of him."

"He told me he was going to drop it through the mail slot when he locked up last night. Maybe it was his way of making sure he remembered to leave it behind. If he left it on his keyring or in one of his piles he'd have probably forgotten."

"Was the victim often forgetful?"

"I'd say so," she agreed.

"And, did you have to unlock the shop when you arrived this morning?"

Bert paused, finally understanding where this line of questioning was taking them. The detective was inferring that Bert might have something to do with this whole murder business.

"Well?"

"Yes, Detective. I did have to unlock the shop."

"I see. Very interesting."

"You're implying that, without a key, the killer couldn't have gotten in and out?"

Caught in his own theory, the detective scowled. "If what you say is true, Mrs. Hannah, then the whole shop was locked up tight. Whoever killed our friend, Mr. Pennyworth, had to have locked up when they left." He held up Brinkley's key one last time. "And they couldn't have done it with this key. Therefore, I must conclude that the culprit either has a key themselves, or borrowed one."

"Are you accusing me?" she blurted.

"No, I'm not. Not yet, anyway."

"I can assure you, I had nothing to do with his death," Bert argued breathlessly.

"What time did you and Mr. Jankes leave?" he asked without skipping a beat.

"Sometime just after nine-thirty."

"And were you two traveling together?"

"No, we walked out the door and went our separate ways."

The detective only nodded as if he'd learned something significant. "Did you notice anything unusual either last night or this morning?"

"You mean like a dead body?" she stated dryly, getting tired of Detective Mannor's pompous attitude.

"There is no need to get an attitude, Mrs. Hannah."

"I'm sorry," she replied firmly and without sincerity.

Mannor went on, unbothered by her slight outburst. "I meant, did you notice anything that was missing, something that may have been there the night before that had suddenly disappeared."

Bert paused, taking inventory of her memory of the office. "Wait. Was there a letter opener on the desk this morning? A long silver one?"

The detective pursed his lips. "No, not that I'm aware of."

Placing her palms flat on the table, she stood up with a start. "Oh, my goodness."

"What is it, Mrs. Hannah?"

"Don't you see? That was the weapon. Someone stabbed him with his own letter opener."

Chapter 7

A fter getting another two cups of coffee in her system, just to keep alert, and eating two donuts, Bert headed back to the bookshop. Thankfully, the police had finished most of their initial walk-through and the coroner had officially taken the body away. A simple police barricade was situated around the doorway to discourage customers from coming inside, but no other measures were deemed necessary at that point. They were getting closer to finishing their work at the crime scene.

They had a wagon parked out in the back alley and were carefully labeling and loading all the significant evidence and boxes from the office. That way they could properly search each one for the murder weapon.

Detective Mannor allowed Bert in the left side of the building where there was the most work to be done. While the detective continued his investigation of the back office on the right side, Bert got down to business organizing books; she needed something to keep herself busy.

The left side of the shop had its fill of shelves, all crowded in and stacked up high. There were, of course, labeled sections, but none of them seemed to be alphabetized by author as was the usual method. Comics, self-help books, and more were all among the many shelves. There was even a cookbook section.

Bert took a few minutes to search the titles for 300 Percent Pies. Unfortunately, she didn't find a copy.

She made a mental note of the space, thinking she'd leave one wall for shelves of books. It could be the new releases and featured titles section of the shop, enticing dessert lovers to pick up a bestseller while they enjoyed some sugary delights.

However, there was a lot to do before she could even think of getting the pie shop up and running.

The first order of business, in her mind, was clearing out the doorway. It was a tedious task, to say the least, as she went ahead and started unloading the floor to ceiling shelf of its contents. She found some cardboard boxes and began stuffing them full of the hefty books.

After some time, the shelf was cleared and ready to be moved aside. Using a rusty hand truck from the crowded stock room, she carefully eased it under the piece of furniture and gently rocked it back, pulling away.

The instant the shelf was moved, a ray of fresh morning sunlight flooded through the glass doors and windows, giving the room a cheery atmosphere where the dim gloom had been moments before. She sighed with a happy satisfaction, receiving her first glimpse of how her shop would turn out, but the moment faded the instant she spotted a woman peering in.

Her face was smashed up against the window, her nose and forehead creating marks on the glass. She had her purse in one hand and a hefty tome of a book under her other. Clearly, she had ignored the plastic orange and white police barricades and stepped in between them to get to the shop.

Before Bert could call out a warning that the shop was closed for the day, Pearl came waltzing through the front door on the right side—which had been left propped open for the police to come and go as they pleased.

"Excuse me, but we're closed today, Pearl," Bert informed her as she approached the woman, passing under the bricked archway which acted as a portal between the two shops.

"Huh?" the old woman mumbled, heading off to look at books like she hadn't heard the new shop keeper. Either that or she was just completely ignoring her.

"Ma'am, the shop is closed," Bert said again, following the woman and tapping her on the shoulder.

The woman let out a surprised squeak and spun around. "What the devil do you think you're doing, scaring an old woman like that?"

"Didn't you hear me? This place is closed."

Clutching her large book closer to her chest, a copy of the complete works of William Shakespeare, Pearl stared intensely. "And who, may I ask, are you?"

"I'm the new owner of this shop, and we're closed."

"New owner?" she blurted out, her eyes widening in utter surprise.

"That's right."

The woman looked around herself in awe, still clearly not having seen the police activity in the back, or the police cars still parked out front. "So, you own everything in here?"

"Yes, and we are closed," she reiterated.

"I was wondering if you could sell me a book," she interrupted, not listening at all to Bert's fourth insistence that they were not open for business.

"No, I cannot."

"It's the copy of Macbeth, the one behind the counter," she motioned toward the book that was still propped up in the same manner as it had been the day before.

"I'm sorry, no."

"I'll give you a hundred for it."

"Ma'am, we are closed, and in case you didn't see, there is an active police investigation going on right now. I'd appreciate it if you'd leave."

The woman's face went slightly pale. "A police investigation? Why? What's happened?"

"There was an accident, that's all," Bert answered, not wanting to get caught up in a long discussion when there was so much work to be done.

"Is someone dead? Is it Mr. Pennyworth?" she asked, absently walking off between the shelves. Clearly, she assumed she would be able to get a glimpse of the crime scene.

"Ma'am, come back here," Bert shouted, following the woman.

Darting in between the shelves, the woman had seemingly disappeared.

"Pearl? Pearl?" Bert called, desperately trying to locate the woman.

Suddenly, she popped out her head from one of the book nooks.

"Ma'am."

"How about this book? How much do you want for it?" she asked, holding up a worn copy of Emma by Jane Austen.

"No, I can't sell you that."

"What about Macbeth? You never gave me an answer."

"I told you, we are closed," she groaned, wanting nothing more than to clear this troublesome customer out and get back to work cleaning up the area where the pie shop would be.

"So, you won't sell me anything?" she gasped, her face going slack as if she was appalled at Bert's lack of customer service.

"What's going on?" Detective Mannor asked as he appeared between the shelves, his large shoulders almost touching both sides of the skinny aisle. Upon seeing Bert, he frowned. "Mrs. Hannah, I believe I told you, you could work on the left side of the shop, but not over here."

"I was, but this nice lady mistakenly came in to do some shopping," she motioned toward Pearl, gritting her teeth at having said nice.

The detective turned to the woman and folded his arms. "Ma'am, did you not see the very clear police barrier we have set up outside on the sidewalk?" he snapped.

"I saw no such thing. I suppose there were a few things in the way that I had to squeeze around."

"The shop is closed for the day, Ma'am, for a police investigation. You'll have to leave."

Pearl's jaw dropped open and she huffed. "Well, why the heck didn't you just say so in the first place?" Setting down the copy of Emma, she dug into her purse and pulled out her orange medication bottle, dropping two little white round pills into her mouth.

"Ma'am, can you please leave?" the detective demanded.

"See what you bring me to? You've made me so anxious that I have to take my emergency heart medication."

"Ma'am, please," the detective insisted, narrowing his eyes at Bert to get rid of the woman.

"I'll be contacting the station and filing a complaint about the way I was treated here today. And you," she jabbed a bony finger into Bert's shoulder, "don't expect me to ever come into this shop again, not while you're the proprietor." Pointing her nose high in the air, she pushed past Bert and made a dramatic exit, not unlike the one from the day before.

"Thank goodness for that," Bert whispered.

Detective Mannor raised a scolding eyebrow at her. "You really need to keep your customers under wraps. Don't let anyone else in," he ordered, stomping off back toward the office.

Bert groaned, letting her shoulders slump in an exhausted gesture. This was turning out to be an overwhelming first day as a business owner.

Chapter 8

Heading back toward the left side of the shop, Bert took note of the copy of Macbeth behind the counter. Picking it up, she gingerly flipped through the pages, examining the yellowed edges and raised ink lettering. It was clearly an old book, likely printed around the turn of the century by the looks of it.

What bothered Bert was, why was the woman so dead set on getting her hands on it?

"I said the left side of the shop," the detective barked at Bert, spotting her stalling at the counter.

Working very hard not to make an angry face or roll her eyes at the overbearing police officer, she walked into the left side of the store, keeping the little hardback book in one hand.

Once out of the Detective's sight, she took a seat on a red Victorian style chair and continued her examination. Opening the cover, she read over the front matter. This particular edition of Macbeth had been published by Bartleby Books, a company she had never heard of. Additionally, her assumption had been correct about the date of publication. This printing was put out in eighteen-ninety-eight.

Realizing just how old it was, she was almost afraid to handle it too much. After all, she had no idea who it belonged to now that Brinkley was dead and gone. It was the only item, as per the contract, that didn't fall into her possession upon taking over the shop, and she doubted it belonged to her now either.

Straining to remember if Brinkley had a wife, children, or any other family, she couldn't come up with any memories of such. As far as she knew, the former shop owner had no one else in the world.

"I wonder if this is worth anything?" she whispered, turning the book over in her hand. If it was, she was sure Brinkley didn't know about it. He may have sold old and out-of-print books, but his business sense wasn't that great. Generally, he just charged two or three dollars for used paperbacks and five to ten for hardcovers.

He likely didn't know how to use a computer and didn't have one in the shop at all. He was old fashioned like that, even used an old manual cash register where you had to punch in every price.

Bert, on the other hand, while not the most tech savvy woman in the world, had taken it upon herself to learn about computers, cell phones, the internet, and all the rest of it as it became popular over the years.

"It's important to keep up with the times," her husband was always saying. He was generally referring to the carpet laying business and the necessity to contact customers over e-mail, text, and other forms of digital communication. Bert, being the one to handle the finances and books, had also learned the latest budgeting software.

On top of all of it, she had grown fond of computer games, though she'd never have told that to any of her friends or peers. She worried they'd think she was batty, but something about getting a perfect score in a game was very satisfying for her.

It was a great stress reliever.

In addition to her own home computer, she also had one of the fancy smart phones that could get on the internet from anywhere.

Pulling out that phone now, she turned it on. It had the largest screen of any phone on the market, which made it easier for her to see whatever it was she was reading.

Glancing at the copy of Macbeth again, she opened her internet browser and began typing some information into the search engine—the book title, the publication date, and the publishing company.

The results that came up astounded her.

On multiple used book websites and other second hand online shops, there were copies of the same book in question. According to the listings, this little book was worth over five thousand dollars. Additionally, there were only twenty-five of these ever printed.

Did that mean that Pearl knew all about the book's real value and was trying to rip Brinkley off? If that were true, Bert was sickened by Pearl's complete lack of any sense of honesty or discretion.

Knowing the true worth of the family heirloom, Bert became determined to get the book into the right hands—whoever that may be.

"There she is," came an insistent woman's voice from the open doorway.

"Oh, heavens. Now what?" Bert exclaimed, hopping up from the chair to stop any more customers from waltzing in.

While the investigative team had dwindled down to only the detective and two extra officers, she wondered why they didn't have at least one officer standing at the front door to stop people from coming in if the detective cared about it that much.

She guessed it was her responsibility as the shop owner, now, to manage it.

"We're closed," she said, walking over to the woman with the permed dark hair standing in the door. Upon getting closer, she recognized the person.

It was Rebecca Stallion, the ornery owner of the Candy Emporium where Bert always bought an ice cream each week. Standing behind her was Kyle Jankes. "Mrs. Stallion, did you not hear me? There are police barriers up," the young landlord protested, trying to get the woman to leave.

"Tell her, Mr. Jankes. Tell her she can't do it," Rebecca charged forward, pointing at Bert with an accusatory finger.

"I will do no such thing, now let's get out of here," Kyle demanded, never leaving the safety of the open doorway.

"Mrs. Hannah," came an angry shout from the back of the building.

All three people turned to face Detective Mannor as he stomped his way to the front of the store.

"Who are these people? I told you that no one else was allowed on the premises. Why have you directly disobeyed my orders?"

Bert had enough, her frustration bubbling to the surface. "Detective Mannor, I have done no such thing. It is not my responsibility to make sure people aren't coming and going as they please. These two have simply waltzed past your police barricade the same as the previous woman. I've had nothing to do with either of these intrusions. In fact, if anyone is at fault it's you for not having a guard on duty."

Mannor paused, taken aback by the woman's outburst. He wasn't used to being spoken to in such a way. "My fault?" he finally blurted out, his face turning red. "I have all of the men available to me, which is only a small handful, working to get things sorted out so that you can have control of your shop back. I thought I was doing you a decency."

"Clearly not, since I seem to be inundated with people who can't stay on the other side of a simple police barrier." She narrowed her eyes at Rebecca Stallion.

The woman's jaw dropped wide open. "Well, I never. How dare you accuse me of such frivolous behavior."

"You walked past the barrier without a second thought, didn't you?" Bert barked, her voice growing louder and louder as she pointed at the very clearly marked plastic signs out front.

"Please, please," Kyle shouted at the top of his lungs, forcing the two women into silence.

They both quieted down, Bert looking embarrassed for her outburst and Rebecca looking infuriated and insulted.

"Now, Mrs. Stallion, I tried to warn you not to step past this barrier, and you have. Now you've not only offended this detective, but you've also upset Mrs. Hannah, my new tenant."

Mrs. Stallion was flabbergasted, her mouth still hanging open as if she were trying to catch flies.

"If anyone is at fault in this little misunderstanding, it's you," he accused her.

Rebecca clamped her mouth tightly shut, her lips squeezing together in a grimace. "My shop has been here longer than you've been alive. I have some right to the decisions that go on at this market."

"Not in the slightest, you don't," he shot back at her, staring her down.

"I don't have to stand here and listen to this." Stomping off, she disappeared back out of the shop and past the police barrier.

"Detective, Bert, I'm truly sorry about this."

"Now, wait a minute, young man," Detective Mannor called. It was a little odd hearing him call Kyle a young man, but Bert supposed, compared to both of them, he was young. After all, he couldn't be older than thirty-five.

"Yes?"

"What is your name?"

"My name is Kyle Jankes. I'm the landlord for most of Old Market."

"The landlord? You seem a bit young."

"I inherited the business from my father and my grandfather, you understand."

"I see. Well, as the landlord, aren't you the least bit interested why there is a police investigation happening on your property?"

He gave a polite nod. "Indeed, I am, Detective, but I assumed that you or one of your men would contact me when it was appropriate and if it was necessary to talk with me."

"Do you have a key to this building?" was the next question past the detective's lips.

"Well, of course I do. I have one for all the buildings I own."

Mannor nodded with a firm determination. "Then, yes, we will need to talk to you. Do you have a moment now?"

"May I ask exactly what it is I'm being interviewed about?" he pressed.

"Murder, Mr. Jankes."

Chapter 9

Bert got quite a bit of work completed while Kyle was in the stock room of the bookstore being questioned. She'd managed to clear out the entire front entrance area of the left side of the shop, creating a clean look that she liked. Things would be wonderful once the pie shop was completely in place and the bookstore reorganized.

Kyle finally came out of the stockroom with the detective not far behind. "Thank you for your time, Mr. Jankes. I will be in contact."

"Let me know if there is anything else I can do," he offered.

Without answering, the detective headed back toward the office again.

Kyle came to stand next to Bert and sighed. "He suspects one of us, you know?"

"I'm aware of that fact," she grumbled, shoving more books into boxes. "We're the only two besides Brinkley who have keys to the building, and when I found the body this morning the whole place was locked up tight. That leaves you and me as the likely suspects."

"I suppose so, but what reason would either of us have for killing the old man?" he asked in a sincere tone.

Bert refrained from mentioning the nine thousand dollars of rent owed. In the end, it hardly seemed like motive enough, since Brinkley had just earned money from selling the business. Killing the man would just mean he was out the money for good.

"Well, I don't have a motive," Bert noted.

"I think that detective is trying to dig one up."

"If he's such a good detective, why not have an officer posted out front so I won't have to field all the psychos who decide to disobey the large signs that say do not cross on them."

"I heard a rumor that our city's force was low staffed," Kyle offered.

"I guess, but that hardly seems like an excuse."

"I mean, we may not be a small town, but we're certainly not the size of some of the bigger cities. We exist mostly for tourists driving through."

"I understand that, I do. I just don't think it's fair that I get blamed for other people's poor choices. I swear, that detective has it out for me."

"Hey, give him a break. He might be a grump, but I've heard of him. He's solved quite a few murder cases in his time."

"He has? Well, maybe he should quit when he's ahead and retire. He may be slipping in his old age."

"The police don't always have someone on watch in situations like this, even in the bigger cities. Believe me, I've traveled enough to see. Usually, having the barricades up is enough for most people."

"Well, it wasn't enough for Rebecca Stallion."

Kyle frowned, folding his arms. "She was upset that I was allowing another food business, specifically sweets and desserts, into the Old Market."

Bert cocked a confused eyebrow. "Why would that matter?"

"She's one of the longest running shop owners in the market and thinks she has some sort of entitlement to all of the choices made. Believe me, I've been dealing with her craziness since I took over for my Pops."

Bert pushed the box she had just filled with books to the side and stood up. "It looked like she was ready to attack me earlier."

"I wouldn't put it past her. She dragged me over to make an official complaint about your pie shop."

"How did she ever hear about it?"

"Carla Young was excitedly telling other shop owners."

"Of course," Bert said with a laugh.

"Anyway, she thinks the competition will hurt her business."

"I don't see how. We sell completely different foods. Heck, I get an ice cream from her almost every week."

"I agree, it isn't a problem, but at least now I can tell her I've discussed it with you. It'll get her off my back for a while, anyway. My assumption is, as soon as you have your grand opening, she'll be back at it again."

Bert smiled at him. "Thanks for the warning."

"No problem," he beamed.

"You know, you seem an awful lot nicer than people let on. I mean, you're a businessman when you need to be, but you also seem very good natured when dealing with people."

He sat in a red armchair, smirking with only half his mouth. "I will admit, Mrs. Hannah, I have a temper."

"Call me Bert."

"It costs a lot of money to run this whole operation. I can get pretty snippy when I feel it's needed. As I did with Brinkley the other night for his overdue bills."

The mention of money reminded Bert of something that had happened the day before, and she wondered if Kyle knew anything about it. "You know, there was another man in here recently who was trying to pump Brinkley for money. He seemed pretty angry, had a slight New York accent."

Kyle scowled. "That'll be Marc Bailey, most likely. He works in investments and is always trying to get the shop owners around here to participate in some project or other. Truth be told, he isn't that great with money and is often taking advantage of some of the more timid people on his roster."

Bert hummed thoughtfully. "You don't think he had anything to do with this?"

"I couldn't honestly say. I don't really interact with the man."

Bert only nodded, thinking about the other possibilities. She just had to figure out a way to clear her name off the suspect list. "Is there another way into this building? Any way at all where you wouldn't need a key?"

"There is a back door, but I assume it's locked."

"Wait a minute." Bert had a sudden idea and walked over to the newly uncovered left side door. She pulled on the handle, but it didn't budge. "Darn. I thought maybe this one had been accidentally left open all this time."

"It was a good thought."

"What about upstairs?" she pointed upward.

"It's technically apartment space, but most shop owners use it as storage. The only door in or out is at the top of the stairs."

"What about the windows? Is there a fire escape on the back of this building?"

"There is, but it's nearly impossible to get up to it from the alley. Someone has to unlatch the ladder from the top to get it to extend down."

"Darn."

"I mean, you can check it all out, but I'm not sure you're going to find much of anything. I suggest letting the police handle it," he stood up, straightening his suit jacket.

"What, so Mr. Gung-Ho Detective can arrest one of us?"

"He is the best in the city. Don't forget that," he pointed out, walking past her to leave.

"I'll believe it when I see it."

Chapter 10

B y two in the afternoon, Bert's energy was all but spent. Between the shocking experience of finding a dead body, dealing with a pompous and overbearing detective, taking on Pearl and Rebecca, and finally shuffling box after box of books around, Bert had worn out any steam left in her as well as the boost from her extra cups of coffee that morning. She needed a serious break and heading back to the cottage for a long candlelit soak in the bath, followed by an evening with some of her favorite British television shows sounded like just the ticket.

Most nights, she liked to read a little before bed, and Victorian literature was her personal favorite. This time, however, she didn't feel like she could look another book in the spine until morning, no matter if it was Stevenson, Poe, or her good friend Dickens.

The drive home was about twenty minutes and it only added to her exhaustion, so much so that she barely felt able to draw her own bath. Somehow, she managed to get the tub filling and a few of her favorite cinnamon and vanilla scented pillar candles, purchased from Christmas in July, lit. They filled the bathroom with a warm ambient glow. Adding some music from the radio app on her phone, the classical station, she slipped out of her jeans and blouse and crawled into the steaming hot water, grimacing against the pain at first but then settling in comfortably.

She knew she should be thinking of something for dinner, but was in no mood for cooking. She figured she'd order something out from the local Italian shop down the road. She didn't often eat out or buy pre-made food, but days like this one called for it.

As she settled back in the water, she closed her eyes and thought of the many ways she could improve upon her new business venture. She already had visions for how it might be decorated.

She loved the dark red of the brick walls and was hoping to build off that theme. She thought of a color scheme involving of deep maroons, earthy browns, rich blacks, and creamy tans or golds. She figured on cherry wood wall paneling with a nice gold trim. Even the glass displays and shelves would be done with wood frames or black metal. She would add hanging light fixtures with soft filter glass shades. Using the armchairs and cushions that Brinkley had left behind she could, create an entire sitting area with tables.

The whole thing, in her mind at least, seemed very Victorian.

It would take a serious investment of money upfront, but if she played her cards right she'd have it all paid off in no time.

Her mind began to wander as she thought of Brinkley again. If that detective got it in his head to try and pursue Bert as the main suspect she could be in trouble. What if he somehow came up with some reason to arrest her? Her happy vision of a pie shop mixed with a bookshop would be drowned before it even started.

She didn't like the sound of it, didn't like it at all.

The stress of the day started to creep back as she considered the options. Surely there was some logical explanation of how someone other than herself or Kyle Jankes got inside the building.

On the other hand, she considered, what was to stop Kyle from being the murderer? After all, there was money owed between the men. What if he'd gone back to the store that same night and asked for his nine thousand right up front, no delays?

What if Brinkley had ultimately refused?

The landlord could have lost his temper, picked up the letter opener, and stabbed him.

Afterward, he might have hidden the bloodied weapon somewhere in the store, somewhere he knew the police wouldn't find it. After all, the building had been in his family for three generations. He probably knew all the intricacies and ins and outs of the place. Maybe there was a secret hiding place?

Bert opened her eyes and stared at the ceiling. What if it had been that Marc person instead? Perhaps the man arrived late that night after both Kyle and Bert had left. He goes inside and demands his money. When Brinkley refuses to pay, Marc does the same thing as in the other scenario, picks up the nearest sharp object—the letter opener—and stabs the poor old man.

Then what? Bert asked herself.

Maybe he took the key and locked up behind himself.

Bert shook her head. That didn't make any sense at all. How would he lock up and then get the key back onto the desk?

It just didn't work.

She thought briefly about Pearl, the incessant customer who wanted the copy of Macbeth for herself. Had she resorted to murder to get the expensive book? It didn't make sense. If it had been the old woman, she would have just taken the book along with her, right? Besides, Pearl was too old and weak to stab someone.

And there was still the trouble with the key.

Bert was at a loss.

Sitting up in the bath, she reached out and grabbed a towel. She was getting hungry and craving pizza. A good Edwardian TV drama and a slice of Hawaiian style might not be a bad combination.

Chapter 11

The next morning, Bert felt like she'd gotten some of her spunk back, as well as some of her excitement about her new business. She decided she'd go back and work a little more on moving books that morning and then start doing research and making phone calls to contractors she could trust to do the remodel. It was going to be a lengthy and involved process, but she wanted to get everything moving as quickly as possible.

If she was efficient in her decisions, she could have the shop open by early October—just in time for the start of the holiday season. That gave her just under two months to get things in order. It was a perfect plan.

Taking some time to cook a proper breakfast, including three strips of turkey bacon, two farmer's market duck eggs, and a whole pile of hash browns, she chowed down. She would need to keep her energy up if she wanted to get her entire list of items done. To top off the morning meal, she had two mugs of steaming hot coffee.

Once she finished eating, and reading the comics from both that day and the previous one, she headed out the door to make the twenty-minute commute to the Old Market. There weren't many large main highways running through Culver's Hood, so driving from one end to the other took a little longer—with slow speed limits through neighborhoods and past schools as well as stop lights.

She arrived in the Old Market around nine-thirty, and pulled up next to a police car parked on the street in front of her shop. "Oh, goodness," she groaned upon seeing Detective Mannor standing in the doorway with his arms folded and his best scowl on.

Hopping out of her car, she approached him. "Can I help you with anything?" she asked in a less than polite voice.

"No, not necessarily."

"Don't tell me you still want to keep everything all cordoned off all day. I've got a business to get up and running."

He held up a hand for silence. "We've got most everything cleared up, Mrs. Hannah. The shop is back in your control for the time being."

"Well, I'm glad to hear that."

"Also, I wanted to stop by and make sure you were doing all right after everything you had to deal with yesterday."

This comment made Bert pause and raise a confused eyebrow. "Is this the same Detective from yesterday?" she asked in all seriousness.

"Mrs. Hannah, when I get on a case I tend to lose myself in a certain frame of mind. I apologize if any of my behavior came off as rude or imposing."

She pursed her lips. "Thanks for that. Now, if you'll excuse me."

"About the whole issue with the guard."

She froze in place, her key poised at the lock.

"At the moment, our force here in Culver's Hood is a little short staffed at times. The chief is actually looking for new officers right now."

"Good for him," she replied in a low voice. She wanted to get on with her day and forget about police procedure and murders for a while.

"Seeing as this wasn't a high-profile murder case, I felt confident in leaving up the police barricade as a method to steer off any unwanted guests. We've used this same method successfully on other occasions. Most people won't dare step inside a barrier when there are police still on the premises. They know better."

"Well, not this time," she pointed out, sliding the key into the lock and turning it.

"It seems you had a few insistent customers, yes."

Bert bit her lower lip to keep from saying something she might regret.

"My point is, I apologize for my poor attitude yesterday. Murder is a serious business and I intend to catch the culprit."

"Well, thanks for coming by to say all that. Good luck on the case," she rattled off quickly, opening the door intending to end the conversation by going inside, an act that annoyed Mannor.

"But don't think I'm going soft. I don't want you getting any funny ideas, you hear me?" He waved a commanding finger, the normal rude attitude she remembered from the day before resurfacing.

"What, like skipping out of town?" she replied with a little hint of fire in her voice.

"You know exactly what I mean. No need to get fresh," he snapped.

"Have a good day, Detective," she offered, stepping inside and preparing to shut the door.

With a flip of his hand, he held out a card. "This has my work and personal numbers on it. Give me a call if you think of any new information concerning the murder. Anything at all."

She paused, taking the card and glancing at it. The personal phone number was scribbled in pen under the printed work information.

"Good day," he grunted, finally taking off.

Bert closed the door and let out a low chuckle. If she didn't know any better, she'd say Detective Mannor was beginning to tolerate her.

Chapter 12

Heading toward the back of the shop, Bert kept her eyes trained on the office door. She was slightly hesitant about going into the same room where a murder had occurred. The image of Brinkley's body flashed in her memory, the small spot of blood soaking his shirt.

She stood reluctantly outside the doorway, yesterday morning's events waiting just beyond the threshold.

Shivering at the thought, she tried to summon up her courage again. After all, there wasn't a dead body in that room anymore and any evidence of such had been removed.

Stepping into the office, she let out a whoosh of relief to find everything quite ordinary. Of course, the desk had been completely cleared of any items—all most likely taken in for evidence—and the desk chair was missing.

Bert wondered if it had bloodstains on it.

Walking around the desk, she set her purse down and began opening drawers. They, too, were all empty. Shrugging, she stored her items in one of the larger bottom drawers and closed it tight.

Standing upright, she shivered slightly, feeling a draft. She rubbed her arms through her jacket, attempting to warm herself.

The gentle brush of air on her face caused her to look about the room inquisitively.

Where was it coming from?

Feeling the draft again, she noticed it coming from above her. Glancing up toward the ceiling, she spotted the vent situated just above the desk.

It was wide open and the air was coming through.

Running out of the room, Bert grabbed a ladder and brought it in, setting it just beside the desk and climbing up until she could reach the high ceiling. Through the slats she could just make out hints of daylight peeking through.

This gave Bert pause.

Hadn't the vent been closed the night Brinkley died?

She was nearly positive it was.

Did that mean the police officers had opened it to air out the room? Or had it been opened by the killer the same night of the murder?

Pulling on the tab, the grate shut closed, echoing loudly.

She was having the strangest idea, a theory that seemed farfetched but could possibly work to help show she and Kyle weren't the only suspects.

Climbing back down, she grabbed her keys and headed back into the main shop. Behind the checkout counter, she climbed the stairs to the second floor. Locating the door into the empty apartment, which was being used as storage, she unlocked it and stepped inside.

The room was filled with old worn out shelves, some boxes of tattered books, old chairs, and other items. Despite all the clutter, it seemed like it could be made into a nice living space with a little work.

Scoping out living spaces, however, wasn't Bert's goal in coming upstairs.

Navigating between all the boxes and furniture, she came to the window, flipped the latch, and threw it open. Just as Kyle had described, there was a fire escape on the back of the building. The black iron structure stood rigid and sturdy against the building.

The window was large enough and low enough to allow Bert to easily step through and out onto the walkway.

There was one flight of metal steps going down to a square opening and another going up to the roof.

Looking down, she realized that the ladder through the opening had been released from its locked position and was extended all the way down into the back alley.

That meant that Kyle had been wrong, and someone could have easily climbed up. But who?

Bert headed down the steps and attempted to raise the ladder back up. It wouldn't budge. The lock was stuck in place, broken, leading her to believe that it had been in that same position for some time.

Peering back up, she wondered how the person had gotten in through the latched windows. The detective had said that the entire building was locked up, doors and windows both.

That led Bert back to her original theory, and she proceeded to climb up to the roof. Climbing over the edge of the short brick barrier, she stood up in the brisk wind. The feeling of a late summer rain was in the air.

Glancing around, she didn't see any easily apparent entrances into the building, but did spot a small metal tower with a vent grate on the top.

That was exactly what she'd been looking for.

Walking over to it, she found a pull tab that was identical to the vent in the office below. She pulled on it and heard a loud clunk as it opened. If she was right in her assumption, that meant both vents could be opened and closed from the roof as well as inside.

Her theory was becoming more and more plausible.

Removing an old key from her keyring—which belonged to a bike lock she'd lost some years earlier—she easily slipped it through the vent slats. Listening as it clunked back and forth, it finally came to a stop.

Now, all that was left was to check her theory.

Quickly shuffling back down the fire escape and into the window, she hurried down the stairs.

Stepping into the office, she gasped. Just as she had suspected, the old bike key lay there in the center of the desk, just as Brinkley's shop key had been the morning before.

Chapter 13

"I came as soon as I got your message," Detective Mannor declared, stepping through the front door of the shop without knocking.

Bert was bent over a box of books, organizing them. This whole task of doing a complete inventory was going to take some time. She'd need to clear out a lot of merchandise before she could organize things in the fashion she desired.

"Detective? I wasn't expecting you," she admitted, standing up from her work to greet him with a polite handshake. When she'd called informing him she had some big developments in the murder case, she had expected little more than a phone call back.

Instead, here he stood in the entrance to her shop.

"You did say you had figured out some new information about the murder of Brinkley Pennyworth, correct? I am not mistaken in that fact?"

She raised both hands. "No, no. It's true. I was just surprised that you came all the way back over here."

"You are aware, Mrs. Hannah, that the police headquarters is only a few blocks away from here?"

She offered a timid smile.

He folded his arms. "Now, are you going to tell me what it is you think you've learned, or did I waste my time coming over here?"

"Of course," she answered excitedly. She waved a finger for him to follow.

"This better be good, Mrs. Hannah," he said, putting some of his hardened detective attitude to work.

"Trust me. It is." Stepping into the office, she motioned toward the desk where the bike key sat.

The detective looked at it with a stone expression. "It's a key," he pointed out irritably, not seeing the connection.

"Yes, of course, it's my old bike lock key."

Furrowing his brow, he looked at her with a not too pleased scowl. "You called me down here to show me your bike key."

"Not the bike key, how the bike key got there." She pointed up at the vent.

The detective followed her finger and glanced toward the ceiling, noticing the cool breeze on his face for the first time since entering the office. "The vent is open, I see."

"Exactly."

"Mrs. Hannah, what does any of this have to do with the homicide case?" he demanded, his patience growing thin.

Bert had hoped he could put two-and-two together on his own. She knew that many detectives and officers felt more accomplished when they assumed any given solution was their own idea—especially with men like Detective Mannor.

However, it seemed she would have to spell things out.

"The killer murdered Brinkley and then locked up as they left."

"We've already established this."

"But they used his key."

"How is that possible?"

"They used the fire escape in the alley to climb onto the roof and drop the key through the vent. It fell all the way down onto the center of the desk where you see my bike key now."

The detective's eyes widened as he realized the implications. "You're positive of this?"

"I tested it on my own by dropping this key through. It explains how the killer was able to lock up, but make it look like it could only be committed by someone with a key to the building."

"You wouldn't mind performing your experiment again, would you?"

She snatched up the bike key. "Wait here. I'll be right back."

She dashed up to the roof as quickly as she could manage, dropped the key through the slot, and walked back down again to the office.

The detective held the key in his hand, tossing it up and down. "You were absolutely right," he commended her.

"See, it shows that the murderer could have been anyone," she proclaimed in an exasperated tone, still a little winded from her run.

"This is significant, Mrs. Hannah."

"I know."

"This helps me to pin down a more accurate vision of our murderer," he informed her, the smallest hint of a smile touching the corner of his mouth.

"You think you know who it is?"

"I have my hunches, but it all comes down to motive." He placed the key back on the desk. "I need to get back to the station. I have some important calls to make."

Before he could reach the front door, however, a quiet ring of the bell announced someone's entrance. Bert stepped out to see who it was who had come in, realizing she'd forgotten to lock the door after the detective had arrived.

"Where is he?" demanded the blonde-haired, bearded man.

Bert instantly recognized him as Marc Bailey, the investor.

"Excuse me, but we're closed Mr. Bailey."

"I need to talk to Brinkley Pennyworth," he insisted.

"And who are you?" demanded the detective.

"My name is Marc Bailey, and I need to speak with Mr. Pennyworth."

"Is this about a small matter of money?" Mannor asserted himself.

Marc paused, surprised that this complete stranger seemed to know his business. "As a matter-of-fact, it is. Why?"

"Do you care to share with me your whereabouts between the hours of nine-thirty pm and midnight on the night of August the sixth?"

Marc looked indignantly from the detective to the woman. "What is this?"

Detective Mannor lifted his jacket's lapel and flashed his badge. "Is it true that you wrote Brinkley Pennyworth a threatening letter?"

"What do you mean? Tell me what the heck this is all about?"

"Did you or did you not write a letter demanding money from the previous owner of this shop?"

Seeing he wasn't going to get any answers, he grunted and gave a shrug. "So, what if I did? Am I in trouble or something?"

"I have said letter in my possession at the police station, and if the new information that Mrs. Hannah has provided for me is true, that gives you quite the opportunity and motive."

"For what?" he demanded, his face turning red with a mixture of anger and fear.

"If you wouldn't mind, I'd like you to accompany me down to the station to discuss the recent murder of Brinkley Pennyworth."

In the next moment, Marc went ghostly pale.

Chapter 14

The rest of the day went by in a breeze of work. Thanks to the fact that Marc was the most likely suspect now, Bert felt comfortable to let her worries about being targeted as the murderer go. It made all the hard labor of moving books about more enjoyable.

When she began growing tired in the afternoon, she started making all sorts of notes about the space available and what she hoped to do with it. Using the miracle of internet via her phone, she did some research and made some phone calls to contractors about the best method for remodeling the shop.

She informed multiple companies about her desired vision and got a few different off-the-cuff estimates for the work necessary to bring the dream to life.

She additionally made phone calls to members of her church's congregation, asking if there were any young men or women looking to make a few extra dollars after school each day. Having the helping hands of some vibrant and strong people would make moving all the boxes and creating a proper inventory more accessible.

She also started creating plans of how to thin out the overly stuffed amount of merchandise in the office, storage room, and upstairs apartment. While construction was going on, she knew she could easily hold a street sale to unload much of it for cheap.

She imagined bins of penny style romance and mystery novels, classics, and other books. Selling them for a dollar or less each would be sure to clear out a lot of the unnecessary clutter.

As the sun finally began to set, she realized she hadn't had much of anything to eat since breakfast. Despite having just ordered out the previous day, she called up a local brick oven style pizza shop in the market and ordered some dinner. She gave them instructions to come around to the back door near the office. She would be starting the lengthy process of inventory.

After hanging up, she decided to do a quick walk-through of the right side of the shop and do a preliminary scan of the genres they had in stock. She walked up and down the aisles, making notes of the shelf labels. Approaching the section of Regency and Victorian era fiction, she scanned the titles. Her eyes rested on one that was out of place. "You don't go here," she complained, pulling the large tome from the shelf.

Much to her surprise, the book felt light—too light.

Turning the volume over in her hand, there was an odd clunking sound as if the inside was hollow and something was moving about inside.

"What is this?" she wondered out loud, opening the book.

The pages in the center of the book had been cut out, leaving a square indentation—much like a box—inside. She'd heard of these. They were called hide-away books.

Sitting within the pages was the blood-stained letter opener.

Chapter 15

E agerly digging her phone out of her pocket, Bert dialed Detective Mannor's number again. It went straight to voicemail. "I found the murder weapon hidden in one of the books at the shop, and I think I know who the murderer is. Get down here as soon as you get this," she insisted, hoping she wasn't being too bossy or forward. This was a homicide they were talking about, not some petty theft.

Heading back into the office, she closed the volume and set it on the desk for the detective to take into evidence whenever he arrived. She hoped, by accidentally handling the book, she hadn't somehow incriminated herself or destroyed evidence.

She hadn't touched the letter opener, of course, and that would be the true judge for convicting the murder.

She just hoped the detective would arrive soon.

A heavy-handed knock came from the back door, causing Bert to jump. Her heart pumped at an increased speed for a few seconds before calming down again. "Sheesh," she groaned. She'd been so flabbergasted by finding the weapon, she'd nearly forgotten that the pizza delivery man was on his way.

Grabbing her wallet from her purse, she walked over and opened the door.

Instantly, she felt her blood run cold upon the sight of the person standing outside. It wasn't the pizza guy at all.

"P-Pearl. What are you doing here?"

"I saw the light was on and decided to see if you were in," she admitted.

"What for?"

"We were interrupted during our negotiations," she said, stepping past the threshold without being invited.

"Negotiations?" she asked, trying to keep her voice as calm as possible. Her eyes fell on the book on the desk, praying that Pearl didn't notice it as the same book she'd brought in and hid on the shelf the day before.

"About the book, of course," she demanded.

Bert never knew she could feel as nervous or afraid as she did at that very moment. "The book?" she asked, trying to play dumb and draw out the conversation as long as possible. She hoped that Detective Mannor had gotten her message and would arrive soon.

"The copy of Macbeth. I told you I was willing to pay one hundred dollars for it."

"Now, which copy of Macbeth was that?" she asked stupidly.

"The copy. You know what I'm talking about. The one published in eighteen-ninety-eight."

"It's that old, is it?"

The old woman shook a finger. "As a bookshop owner, you should know these things. Mr. Pennyworth never did, either."

"Oh, I'm sorry. I'm still a little new at all of this."

"Anyway, the point is, I've spent the whole day today trying to scrounge up some extra cash and I'm ready to up my offer to two-hundred dollars." She lifted the cash from her purse.

The woman's pitiful and dishonest offer agitated Bert's sense of justice. "Two hundred for a five-thousand-dollar book?" she blurted out before she realized what she was saying. Instantly, she regretted the words, biting her lips closed.

Pearl paused, her face becoming grim with irritation. "So, I guess you figured it out, huh?"

Sighing, she nodded. "I just couldn't understand why you were so eager to get your hands on it, so I looked up the real value."

"How inconvenient," she sneered, shoving the cash back into her purse.

"I assume it's something Brinkley never knew since he wasn't exactly computer savvy."

"No, he was just stubborn. Family heirloom, he said."

"Why didn't you just take the book when you left the shop?" she asked, stepping into dangerous territory. Her morbid curiosity had gotten the better of her.

The woman tilted her head with surprised eyes. "Whatever do you mean?"

Bert swallowed hard, worrying she'd said too much. "You were here Friday night, correct? To see Mr. Pennyworth about the book?"

"I haven't the faintest idea what you're talking about."

"You overheard, maybe from my friend Carla, about how I was planning to purchase the business. You assumed that Brinkley would take the book with him if he left, so you assumed that was your final chance to get your hands on it."

The woman's lip twitched nervously. "You're wrong. I never came near the place."

"You didn't show up after you saw me and Mr. Jankes leave?"

"No, I did not," she snapped, her knuckles turning white as she clutched her purse.

"And you didn't come in here, offering again to buy the book?"

"No."

"When he refused, you lost it. Without thinking, you picked up the letter opener from his desk and jammed it into his chest."

"No!" she screamed at the top of her lungs.

"The same weapon you hid in the book you brought into the shop yesterday?"

"No, no, no." The woman was frantically digging in her purse, retrieving her medication bottle. Tipping the bottle, the one remaining pill toppled onto the floor, rolling to Bert's feet. "See what you've done?"

Leaning down, Bert picked it up. The little white pill suddenly sparked her memory. She'd seen this somewhere before. In all the items the detective had collected from the desk—the keys, the change, the gum—the thing they had both mistaken as a mint was actually one of the woman's pills.

"I bet these cost quite a lot of money, even with the help from insurance."

"Give me back that pill."

"Is that why you've been trying to get ahold of that book? You could turn around and sell it for thousands."

"I need my medicine," she exclaimed, tears coming to her eyes.

Bert's eyes lowered to the poor woman. "That's it, isn't it?"

"How do they expect a woman of my age, with pitiful retirement and no job, to pay for this kind of thing?" she groaned. "Oh, they think you're in good health just because you can get around without a cane or walker, that you're not totally dependent on someone else, but I'm not."

"You hoped you could make some quick, easy money by buying and reselling that rare book."

"I-I didn't mean for it to happen. I was just so desperate for the money, and when that stubborn old man wouldn't give the book to me, I finally went into a blind rage. It was like I wasn't even myself. I picked up that letter opener and jammed it into him." She shook her head, her hands shaking. "The next thing I knew, he was dead. I panicked, grabbed his key, and ran out of the shop. I locked the door behind me."

"You didn't even think to grab the book, the whole reason you came in."

"I was afraid. Once I was outside, I realized I had the key."

"And you've been to this shop so many times throughout the years, you knew a lot about the building."

"I climbed up the fire escape to the roof and dropped the key back down inside through the vent."

"And then you came back the next day, hoping I'd sell the book to you."

"I didn't know what else to do…" she paused as a knock came at the door.

"That's going to be the detective," Bert noted.

"Detective?" her voice wavered.

"You'll want to tell him what you told me," she instructed her, going to let him in. Opening the door, she was surprised to see Detective Mannor standing there with a pizza box in his hands.

"Hope you don't mind, but I took the liberty of paying for your pizza," he grunted.

Chapter 16

"And here we are. The very first pie baked here in the Pies and Pages bookstore," Bert announced, setting the steaming apple pie down on the table in front of Carla and Kyle. They were sitting at the corner table, an antique piece crafted out of wrought iron and heavy oak. A fringed maroon tablecloth draped over it.

The workers had completed the remodel of the left side of the shop just the day before, transforming it from a humble room into an exquisite pie shop modeled after the Victorian style. They had even put in a false iron door to make the brick wall beside the counter look like an old-fashioned oven.

During the winter months, the door would heat up, warming the patrons as they ate and read.

"Oooh, it's just beautiful," Carla beamed.

The pie itself, made from only fresh ground flour and the crispiest of farmer's market apples, was a work of art. The golden-brown lattice work across the top glistened with the sparkle of melted sugar, and the scent of cinnamon and apples penetrated every corner of the room.

"And you did it without your cookbook? I'm surprised."

Bert shrugged. "As a business owner, I've got to learn to be a little more flexible. Besides, I figured, now that I own a bookstore, why not write a cookbook myself?"

Carla clapped her hands. "Ooh, it's a lovely idea."

Kyle rubbed his hands together. "I can't wait to get a taste of this."

Setting out two acrylic plates, each designed with embellishments to imitate fine china, Bert sliced and served the pie. The caramelized apple filling glistened as she plated it.

Carla was the first one to take a bite, her lips squeezing together in glee as she savored the flavor. "Oh, my. You've really outdone yourself, Bert."

"Let me be the judge of that," Kyle scolded jokingly, digging in and shoveling the first bite into his mouth.

"Well, what's the verdict? Do I have my landlord's approval?"

Kyle waited a moment while he finished enjoying the bit of apple pie he'd just eaten. Finally, he lifted his fork. "I think I made a wise choice allowing your business here in Old Market."

Bert clasped her hands like a delighted schoolgirl. "Fantastic."

"I can't wait for the grand opening," he admitted.

Bert took a seat, setting down a third plate and serving herself a slice. "Well, that won't be for another week and a half, at least. There is still a lot of work to do. I have to move some shelves in here to the pie shop and make sure they're filled with the new releases I ordered, and I have to continue cleaning out that cluttered apartment and the storage rooms, too. I want it to feel cozy, but not too cluttered. I'm shooting for the first of October as opening day."

She had yet to do her street sale to thin out her merchandise but figured she'd have to do it this next week, or wait until the shop was officially open.

"I'll leave my calendar open," he admitted, shoveling another delicious bite of pie into his mouth.

"I can't imagine a better way to begin fall than with a warm apple pie," Carla admitted.

"It is the first day of autumn, isn't it?" Bert proclaimed, remembering it was now the twenty-second of September. The remodel had flown by in a blur, despite it having taken nearly seven weeks. Luckily, during all that time, she'd been sorting books, organizing shelves, and getting the bookshop prepared for the grand opening. However, there were still tasks to be done before October.

Still, she was thrilled. She preferred colder weather to the hot days of summer.

"Yep, and my busy season." Carla finished her last bite.

"Do you want another?"

"Yes, please," she smiled.

Bert dished it out. "I just hope I can get the hang of running a business and survive the holidays at the same time."

"Oh, you'll do fantastic. People will be clambering to get a warm treat while they're out doing a little holiday shopping. You know, you should do hot chocolate and apple cider with the pies, too."

"Whoa, one step at a time. I have to make sure I've got everything under control first," Bert said.

"Maybe in the future, then," Carla suggested.

"Maybe, yes."

"So, have you seen much of that detective since you caught the killer?" Carla pressed, wiggling her eyebrows and cutting into her second slice.

"Not really. I'm sure he's busy with other things. Why?"

"I don't know, based on what you said, it seemed like he sort of liked you."

"Liked me? He couldn't stand me. Half the time we were butting heads."

"That's how it always starts," she sing-songed.

"She's right, you know," Kyle added.

"Oh, what do you know? You're too young."

"I say it how I see it," he said.

"Besides, I'm not interested in anything like that. I could never be with anyone else besides Howie. Also, I'm too busy with my new business."

"I still say he likes you," Carla offered her opinion, munching on another bite.

"I sure hope not. I don't think we would get along." She paused a moment, thinking about the bullheaded, irritating, and pompous detective. "Although, he did pay for my pizza. The least I can do is make him a pie, I suppose."

Made in the USA
Coppell, TX
07 December 2020